17

BLAZING
BLUE

HILDA OFFEN

BLAZING BLUE

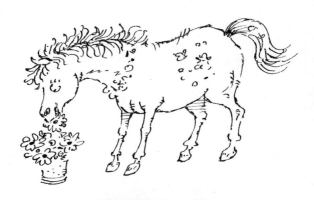

rbP

Ragged Bears Publishing

Published by Ragged Bears Publishing Ltd.
Unit 14A, Bennetts Field Industrial Estate,
Southgate Road,
Wincanton,
Somerset BA9 9DT, UK

First published 2011
1 3 5 7 9 10 8 6 4 2

Text and illustrations copyright © Hilda Offen, 2011

A CIP catalogue record for this book is available from the British Library

ISBN 978 1 85714 426 0
Printed in Poland

www.raggedbears.co.uk

For Jeanne Williams

chapter 1

I was in a strop and I couldn't snap out of it.
Everything seemed to be going wrong.

First of all there was the heat. Too hot for
school. I hadn't been able to think straight. I
trailed along behind Gran and Tommy; every so
often Tommy would try to burst the tar bubbles
on the road with his toe and Gran would yank
him back onto the pavement.

And then there was the new girl, Venetia Best.
Everyone in the class seemed to think she was
the bee's knees – even my best friend, Alice.

"She's got a *pony*, Moo!" whispered Alice

in class. "He's called Sultan. They keep him in stables up on the Downs."

"So?" I said.

"She says she'll take some of us up to see him!" said Alice in a dreamy voice.

Big deal! I didn't like the look of Venetia Best. There was something about the way she smirked at me, as though she knew a secret that she was keeping to herself for the time being. No. Venetia Best definitely got a big Thumbs Down from me. And that went for her pony, too.

We were almost home – and that was another thing. It wasn't our home at all, it was Gran's. Franklin Heights rose above us, red and angry-looking. In fact, it looked exactly like I felt.

Well – you'd feel angry if you'd been abandoned by your parents, wouldn't you? Deserted. *And* forced to live with your grandmother *and* share a bedroom with your little brother.

And then there was the worst thing of all – my name. What were my parents thinking of? (I know what they *say* they were thinking of, but I don't believe them.) I think they just peered down at their new little baby and said:

"What shall we call her? What's the worst name we can think of? How can we blight her life forever? Oh – I know! We'll call her –"

My Gran turned round.

"Come on!" she called. "We're almost there! Don't dawdle, Cowslip!"

Chapter 2

How can everything be so all right one minute and so all wrong the next? I could remember *exactly* the moment when things changed.

I was chasing Tommy round the garden with Mum and Dad. We were a herd of triceratops and Tommy was a small stegosaurus. He was darting round the flowerbeds and shrieking with laughter.

"Got you, Tommy!" I yelled and pounced; and that's when Mum's mobile rang.

I was tickling Tommy now and he was rolling around the grass, shouting and gasping.

"Ssh, Tommy!" said Mum. "Hallo? Oh! Yes – yes! Thank you!"

Then she rushed at Dad, screaming, "We've got it! We've got it!"

Got what?

It turned out that Mr Lowe, the man they'd met at the marina, had asked them to crew for him on his yacht.

"He's flying us out to the Indian Ocean to join the *Mary Ellen*!" screamed Mum, jumping up and down. "Dad's doing the navigation and I'm doing the cooking! They'll love my chickpea lasagne!"

"Cool!" I said. "When do we leave?"

"Oh, Cowslip," said my mum, calming down. "You've got school. You and Tommy can stay with Gran – you'll love it and she'll love having you."

What? I stood there with my mouth open. How could any parents be so selfish?

"It's been our dream to do something like this," said Mum in a pleading voice. She must have noticed my face. "If we don't do it now we never will. We'll send lots of e-mails – I promise."

"We'll be back before you know it," said Dad.

Then Tommy spoke.

"Can I take my dinosaurs to Gran's?" he asked.

And that was all he said.

I was remembering that day as we whirred upwards in the lift. "I hope Bobby Six is all right," said my Gran. "He misses me when I'm out."

Bobby Six is Gran's budgie, a scruffy little green and yellow bird. Gran just loves him to death.

I didn't answer.

"Cheer up, Cowslip," said Gran. "Mum and Dad have been gone for a month already. The time will go quickly, you'll see."

Oh yes? There was another three months to

go. Three *months*! "I wish they'd come back now," I said.

"If wishes were horses," said my Gran.

What did she mean? She was always coming out with things like that.

Clunk! We'd reached the top floor. The doors opened and we walked along the corridor.

We had to wait for ages while Gran fumbled for her keys. The minute she got the door open, Bobby Six set up a delighted chirruping.

"Have you missed me, darling?" asked Gran, poking a bit of cuttlefish through the bars of his cage. "Who's Mummy's good boy, then?"

"Good boy! Good boy!" whispered Bobby.

Ugh! Gran put the telly on and Tommy disappeared into the bedroom to play with his dinosaurs. Time for me to disappear.

chapter 3

I wandered back outside into the corridor. Apart from the bathroom, it was the only place I could be alone. I pressed my nose to the window and stared down at the town.

I could see our house from here. It stood out from all the white, cream and grey houses around it because it was bright yellow. You couldn't miss it.

"*Your* colour, Cowslip," my mum used to say.

And then she'd give me her version of my naming day. How it was just before I was born. How she and Dad were still living in the camper van and had driven up onto the Downs for a picnic.

"And there were cowslips everywhere," said my mum in a soppy voice. "It was like sitting in a sea of gold. I knew there and then – and I said to Dad, 'Let's call her Cowslip'. And your dad said, 'Right on, Babe!' – didn't you, Dave?"

"Um!" grunted my dad, hunched as usual over his navigation charts.

So. Just my luck. They couldn't have chosen a field of daisies to sit in, could they? Or poppies? Or even roses? I could almost hear my mum's voice.

"And then," she was saying, "after you were born, Grandad Cotton left us the house and as soon as we moved in, we painted it. For you."

Thank you, Mum. Thank you, Dad.

I stared down at our house. Mum and Dad had rented it out to another family. There was some washing on the line and I could see a boy riding a bike up and down the path – *my* path.

Hang on! *My* bike! I'd thought it was locked

in the shed. I felt angrier than ever.

I thought about my little garden. The one Dad had dug for me. My flowers would be out by now. I imagined some strange boy or girl sniffing them. Or picking them. I felt as though

I was going to explode. I closed my eyes tight and turned away from the window.

When I opened them again I found I was looking at a flight of stairs at the end of the corridor. At the top was a heavy wooden door. I hadn't really noticed it before.

I stamped up the stairs and pushed, but it

wouldn't budge. There was a keyhole, but no key. I tried to look through it but it was all gunged up.

Then I noticed the cat-flap. It was sealed with sticky tape. I kneeled down, peeled away the tape and pushed. The flap swung open; I had to claw layers of cobwebs out of the way before I could see anything.

And then I caught my breath. I felt excitement bubbling up inside me. I saw a flat roof, a brick wall and railings. There were old flowerpots lying around and even a rusty trowel.

It was a garden! A roof garden! How could I get out there?

"Gran!" I shouted, running back into the flat. "You never said there was a roof garden."

Gran looked up.

"Oh – old Mr Jenkins down the hall used to

take care of it," she said. "It's been locked up for years now."

"Where's the key?" I asked.

"Oh, I've no idea," said Gran, turning back to the TV. "No-one goes on it now. It's too dangerous."

I'd got to get out there! I needed that garden. I needed it desperately. I went back to the corridor and searched everywhere − window sills, door ledges, the steps. But there was no sign of a key. After a while I gave up.

I stamped back into the flat. In the bedroom Tommy was playing with his dinosaurs. They were arranged all over his bed and across the floor. He'd drawn a chalk line down the middle of the room and written a notice on a piece of card. It said 'No wun cros this line'.

"Grr! Roar!" said Tommy, picking up a tyrannosaurus rex and waggling it at me.

"Oh − get lost, Tommy!" I snapped and threw

myself on my bed. Why was I being so horrible to everyone? I wanted someone to step in and say, "Hold on! Stop it right there, Cowslip!" But no-one did.

And from then on, things got worse. I just kept making one mistake after another.

chapter 4

It was Saturday afternoon and I was alone in the flat. Gran had taken Tommy to see Mrs Everett's son on the floor below. Kevin Everett was on the internet and Mum and Dad had arranged to send him e-mails from time to time. It was nice to have the place to myself. I knew Gran would be gone for ages – she usually had several cups of tea and a good gossip with Mrs Everett.

I wandered over to the window. A warm breeze blew in from the open section at the top; I felt it ruffling my hair. I could see the sea and the waves sparkling in the sunshine. Over to my right was the pier; and to my left, I could just make out the marina, its arms stretching out into the blue water.

I used to like the marina. Mum and Dad took us there a lot – to the cinema, to go bowling, or just to have a pizza. But what Mum and Dad were really there for were the boats. It was there that they'd first got chatting to the man who owned the *Mary Ellen.* I wished they'd never met.

Behind me, Bobby Six was chirping away fit to burst. I turned and glared at him. I really hated that bird. If it hadn't been for him, we wouldn't be here, would we? Gran could have come to our house. But –

"Oh no, Cowslip!" said Mum. "She can't leave Bobby Six, can she?"

Bobby Six's cage was enormous. It was built into one side of the room. I went on glaring through the bars. Bobby Six lived in a sort of Bird Palace. Gran had provided him with everything a bird could possibly want. He had cuttlefish and grain and water feeders. He had tiny ladders and plastic toys and all sorts of sparkly things that hung from the cage roof. "Who's a pretty boy, then?" lisped Bobby Six, pecking at a mirror.

Next to the mirror dangled some old Christmas decorations, a bell, some spoons, a row of assorted keys. ... hang on! A row of keys? I stuck my nose through the bars and stared. There were some yales and several ordinary keys. But it was the biggest key of all that caught my eye. It looked the right size. Yes, definitely. But it couldn't be, could it? Could it?

I looked around. Then I unlatched the cage door, thrust in my hand and grasped the key.

And that's when disaster struck. There was a flutter of wings and, to my horror, Bobby Six flew past me. It was all over before I had time to do anything. Bobby Six darted around the room in a panic, bumping into mirrors and chairs and then he was off. He made a bee-line for the open window.

Once he was out, he moved like a rocket. I watched as he shrank to a tiny dot in the blue sky. Then he was gone. I stared at the empty cage. Whatever was I going to tell Gran? I was so struck by the awfulness of what I'd done that it took a few minutes before I realised I was still holding the key in my hand.

I looked at it. Could it be the one? It seemed the right size. Bobby Six was gone now. "No use crying over spilt milk," as Gran would say. I might as well go and try the key in the door.

It fitted! But that was about it. I struggled and struggled, but I just couldn't turn it. It must have been all that gunge in the key-hole. All of a sudden I heard footsteps

on the stairs. I shoved the
key in my pocket and turned
to face Gran and Tommy as they
came round the corner. Tommy was
waving a piece of paper.

"We've got an e-mail!" he shouted.

"What are you up to, Cowslip?" asked
Gran.

"Oh – nothing," I muttered, feeling awful.

I watched as they went into the flat.

I heard Gran say:

"Bobby Six?"

Then there was silence, followed by a long
wail. Gran came rushing out.

"Cowslip!" she cried. "What's happened to
Bobby?"

"I don't know," I lied. "Isn't he there?"

"No!" cried Gran. "Come and help me
look."

We searched the flat. But, of course, there

was no sign of Bobby Six anywhere. I felt worse
and worse.

"Have you been fiddling
with the door, Cowslip?"
asked Gran.

"No!" I lied again. "It can't
have been shut properly."

And that was that. Gran sank into her chair
and stayed there, staring at a framed photo of
Bobby Six. Every so often she'd give a loud sniff
and say:

"Poor Bobby! Poor Bobby Six!"

Tommy disappeared into the bedroom and
I picked up the e-mail. As usual, it was from a
place I'd never heard of.

"Darlings!" it said. "We've seen dolphins! Dad's
navigation's right on course and everyone loves
my cooking! All the best, Mum and Dad."

Chapter 5

Sunday was a miserable day. Gran hardly spoke a word as she clattered around the kitchen getting breakfast.

"You could get a new budgie, Gran," said Tommy. "You could have my pocket money."

"Thanks, Tommy," said Gran. "But Bobby Six was special. No – there'll never be a Bobby Seven."

After a while Gran went down to see Mrs Everett. She took the photo of Bobby with her and Kevin said he'd put it on the internet. He also printed up a lot of small posters, with the photo of Bobby Six at the top and Gran's telephone number. Underneath it said:

"Lost! Small green and yellow budgerigar. Answers to the name of Bobby Six. Any sightings, please call the above number *immediately*."

So we spent most of Sunday trudging around the town in the heat, sticking posters to telegraph poles and lamp-posts, and persuading shop-keepers to put them in their windows.

"I'll never close the window again," said Gran as we rode upwards in the lift.

"Not even if it rains and hails and thunders?" asked Tommy.

"No," said Gran. "It stays open until Bobby Six comes back."

Once she'd managed to get the door open, Gran flopped down in her armchair and turned on the TV. She clasped Bobby's photo to her chest. Tommy disappeared into the bedroom to play with his dinosaurs.

Now was my chance! I borrowed one of Gran's knitting needles and crept out into the corridor. I tip-toed up the stairs and started to poke away at the key-hole. All sorts of grot fell out – dust and dead spiders mostly. It worked, though. Soon I could see daylight. I took the key from my pocket and tried again. Success! This time there was a rusty click and the key turned in the lock.

I pushed the door and it creaked open.

I stepped through. I was standing on a big flat roof, paved with grey mossy tiles. One or two chimney things rose from it; the door I'd come through was in the side of a small block-house.

It was a bit of a mess. There were flower-pots all over the place; lots of them had cracked and

crumbled into heaps. Old dead plants, brown and dry, still poked up from some of them. There were feathers everywhere and all sorts of yukky things the gulls had dropped – chicken bones and pieces of bread and stuff like that. I'd had a faint hope at the back of my mind that Bobby Six might be lurking about up here – but no, there wasn't a sign of him.

I walked all the way round by the railings, deciding the first thing I'd do was have a clear-up. I could see the whole town from here; it shimmered in the heat.

I spread my arms and spun round and round until I felt dizzy. Then I dropped to the moss and lay there, looking up at the sky. It was so blue. I stared and stared. Suddenly a strange

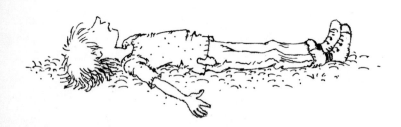

thing happened. High above me the sky began to *fizz*.

Everything went quiet. The sound of the traffic below died away and the swifts stopped squealing. I kept staring. It was as though a giant cloud of midges was gathering in the sky. It was coming closer – closer – then, suddenly, the fizzing stopped and I heard the sound of the traffic again. The swifts were still squealing.

I lay there for a while without moving. I felt strange. I dreamed about getting our house back. About being the most popular girl in the class. About having another name. Jessica … Chloe … Sophie. …

The sun dipped behind the building. I stretched and scrambled to my feet. Time to do my homework. I went back through the door, locking it carefully behind me.

chapter 6

I suppose it had been a bit of a mixed weekend, with a high spot and a low spot. The high spot was that I'd found the key. The low spot was that I'd let my Gran's precious budgie escape. I decided to concentrate on the high spot; I felt almost cheerful. That didn't last long, though.

The first thing I saw when I got to school was a little gaggle of boys and girls surrounding Venetia Best. That didn't put me in the best of moods. Alice saw me and waved.

"Moo!" she cried, running over. "Moo! Guess what?"

"What?" I asked sulkily.

"We've been to see Venetia's *pony*!" cried Alice.

"Me and Lizzie and Tara. He's thirteen hands high, Moo!"

"Thirteen hands?" What did that mean? I knew nothing about horses or ponies. The nearest I'd got to one was a My Little Pony someone had given me for my fifth birthday.

"And, Moo!" went on Alice. "You should see Venetia riding him! She does jumps! She goes over gates!"

"Oh – wonderful!" I said, trying to sound as sarcastic as possible.

"Yes, it really is, Moo!" said Alice. "And that's not all. Sylvia and Simon drove us up there in the Range Rover."

"Sylvia and Simon?" I asked.

"Oh – they're Venetia's parents!" said Alice. "That's what she calls them – and they asked us to call them that too. Anyway, Moo, afterwards they drove us back to their house. And guess what?"

"She lives in a palace?" I said.

"Almost!" cried Alice. "How did you know? She lives in a castle!"

"It's not exactly a castle," said Lizzie, who had been edging towards us. "It's an enormous house with a turret at one end."

"Well, yeah," said Alice. "But the thing is —" she grabbed my arm — "the thing is, Venetia's bedroom is at the top of the turret. Moo, it's brilliant. It's all black, with purple curtains. And you'll never guess what she sleeps in!"

"A bed?" I said.

"No!" shrieked Alice. "A coffin! Venetia sleeps in a *coffin*! Sylvia and Simon asked her what sort of bed she'd like and that's what she asked for — a *coffin*! It's lined with purple velvet and she's got a black duvet. It's so *cool*, Mo!"

"Cool?" I said. I felt really cross. "It

sounds seriously weird to me."

We were interrupted by Venetia.

"Alice!" she called. "Come on!"

"What's the matter with you, Moo?" asked Alice. "You're no fun these days – did you know that? You're so grumpy."

I made a face at her.

"Alice!" called Venetia again.

And guess what? My best friend ran off without a backwards glance. She linked arms with Venetia and they sauntered off into school together. They were giggling and nudging each other; as they went through the door, Venetia looked back over her shoulder and gave me one of her smirks.

Things got worse at lunch-time. I was sitting at the same table as Venetia. I watched as she opened her lunch-box. What was she going to take out? Pheasant? Caviare? (I didn't know what caviare was, exactly, but I knew rich people ate it.)

"So you're called Cowslip," said Venetia, biting into what looked like a salad sandwich. "That's a funny name."

"So?" I said.

"We call her Moo!" said Alice, who was sitting next to Venetia.

"Or Cow!" yelled Alec Johnson, from the other end of the table.

"Pipe down, Alec!" said Mrs Potts the dinner lady, waving her ladle at him.

"Do you know what 'cowslip' means?" asked Venetia, leaning forward with a strange smile.

I took a bite out of my marmite sandwich.

"Of course. It's a flower," I said.

"Wrong!" crowed Venetia, a look of triumph on her face. Everyone was listening now. "It means a cow-pat."

I looked blank.

"It means cow's poo!" hooted Venetia. "My father told me. Ha! Ha! That's what  we should call you – 'Poo', not 'Moo'."

Everyone fell about laughing. And that was that. By the end of the day it had caught on and everyone was calling me 'Poo' – even Alice.

"Bye, Poo-face!" sniggered Venetia, as we crossed the playground after school. She turned to Alice and Lizzie.

"Would you like to come up at the weekend?" she asked. "I'm taking Sultan over the jumps again. I have to practice for the Horse Show."

"Ooh, yes, Venetia!" twittered Alice and Lizzie.

That was what did it. I just couldn't stand it any longer.

That's when I made my Big Mistake.

"I've got a horse!" I said.

They all turned to stare at me. Alice's mouth had dropped open.

"Moo," she began. "You know you –"

But Venetia butted in.

"*You?*" she said. "*You*, Poo-face? You've got a *horse*?"

"Yes!" I said, really angry now. I almost believed it myself.

"And where do you keep it?" said Venetia. "You live in that block of flats, don't you? I suppose you keep it in your bedroom."

And with that she gave another snigger and ran off up the road to where a big black Range Rover was waiting for her.

Chapter 7

If I'd kept a diary, here's how it would have looked for the rest of the week.

TUESDAY: *Alice refuses to speak to me. I hate Venetia Best – or Venetia Beast (my secret name for her). All the kids call me 'Poo'. Miss Grant reads out Venetia's story in Literacy. Gives it ten out of ten and says 'it's very well written'. I borrow some of Gran's pot plants and take them up to the roof garden without her noticing. Borrow a broom, too, and sweep up. Think I can see Venetia's house from here. It has a very small tower at one end.*

WEDNESDAY:

Things get worse at school. People keep asking if they can come up and see my horse. Someone's done a

cartoon and slipped it into my maths book. It shows me and Gran and Tommy all sitting round a table with a horse. Venetia comes top in the maths test.

I find a tap on the roof garden. I manage to get it to turn and rusty water comes out. I water the plant pots. Perhaps something will sprout.

THURSDAY: A small boy called Brian says he'll be my

friend and call me Cowslip if I promise to dance with him at the school disco. I say, "Get lost, Big Ears!" and he puts his tongue out. Says, "I only asked you because no-one else will." Then he runs away. Cheek.

Swimming lesson at the Town Baths. Venetia does the crawl, backstroke and breaststroke. Micky Grimshaw says, "Cor! she moves like a torpedo!" I mutter, "Huh! More like a haddock."

I buy a pot of marigolds and a tray of Busy Lizzies on the way home with some of my birthday money. Gran thinks they're for my room.

FRIDAY: Driven mad by Alice, Lizzie and Tara wittering on about Venetia's pony. Venetia says, "Why don't you hack up to the Downs on your horse, Poo? We could go for a ride together."
The others giggle. I treat them with contempt. It's hotter than ever. Gran asleep so go up to roof and water plants. Can see children in our garden climbing up to our tree-house. Grrrr!

I HATE VENETIA

Chapter 8

I was glad when Saturday came, I can tell you. I couldn't wait for Gran to fall asleep; Tommy was already off in another world with his dinosaurs.

The roof garden looked tidier now. The flowers brightened it up; the only thing was, I needed about a hundred times more. And they were wilting, although I'd watered them once already.

I lay on a beach-towel and gazed at the blue sky. I was really bothered about the horse thing. I wished I'd never said it now. I began to day-dream. It was a good place for day-dreaming.

In my day-dream I really did have a horse.

He was twenty hands high – much bigger than Venetia's. And one day I'd ride him to school and into the playground and everyone would be amazed. And then I'd jump the playground fence and gallop off and that would be one in the eye for you, Venetia.

High above me the seagulls whirled, their wings lit by the sun. I felt the hot roof beneath my body and above me the sun blazed – it blazed like a furnace. And I couldn't believe how blue the sky was. It was a deep, deep blue. I felt as though I was being drawn up into it.

"Blue!" I chanted. "Blue, blue, blue."

Then, just because I liked the sound of it, I yelled:

"BLUE! BLUE! BLUE!"

And that's when it happened. Though I don't suppose you'll believe me. Please yourself. The sky began to fizz again and all the sounds around me died away.

Slowly the blue midges began to take on a shape – a shape that whirled round and round, growing bigger all the time. I sat up, hardly able to believe what I was seeing.

It was a horse – a blue horse. Blue like the sky. And this horse came sailing towards me and landed delicately on the roof.

"You called?" it said.

I scrambled to my feet. I couldn't speak.

"You called?" said the horse again; and then, as I still didn't answer, it stamped a hoof impatiently and said:

"Cat got your tongue? I asked you a question – did you call me?"

"I don't know," I stuttered at last.

"I distinctly heard my name," said the horse. " 'Blue'. Short for 'Blazing Blue'. That was you, I suppose?"

"Yes," I said.

The horse pranced around before me. It waved

and shimmered and from time to time I caught sight of the railings through its body.

So here it was. My dream horse. And I have to say I was seriously disappointed. The horse in my day-dream had been a noble creature – dark and glossy and a bit of a star. This horse, this Blazing Blue, was none of those things. It was small and scruffy and, above all – blue. Quite honestly, it looked a bit silly as it pranced around before me, its mane waving from side to side and its long eyelashes fluttering. It reminded me of something. Hang on! I knew what it was. It was My Little Pony.

"You look as though you could do with some cheering up," said the horse.

It rose up on its hind legs and started to do a sort of tap dance around the roof. It leapt onto the block-house and beat out a tattoo with its hooves.

"Guess what tune this is," it said.

I just stood there with my mouth open.

"It's 'Twinkle Twinkle Little Star'," said the horse. "Come on – buck yourself up."

Then it leapt from the block-house to the railings and balanced its way all round the roof. It ended by leaping down in front of me, whirling round and round and doing a double somersault. It fell back on its bottom, put its head to one side and looked at me.

"Well?" it said. "No applause?"

I clapped in what I hoped was a sarcastic way.

"Louder, please," said the horse.

I clapped again, looking sulky.

"You seem a very *grumpy* girl," said the horse.

I said nothing.

"Why don't you tell me what's up?" said the horse.

And to my amazement I found myself reeling out my troubles – my parents going away, having to leave the house, Venetia Best, letting Bobby out, Venetia Best, the horse story, Venetia Best …

"And then there's this," I finished up, waving my hand. "I wanted to turn this into a beautiful garden, but I'll never do it – just look at it."

The horse turned its head and looked at the limp flowers. Then it absently-mindedly started to nibble at the marigolds.

"Oi!" I said.

"Don't worry," said the horse. "Watch this!"

And it started to do another dance. But this time – this time, every time its hooves struck the ground, flowers appeared. Blue flowers. Blue flowers sprouted from the tiles, blue flowers raced along the railings and blue dangly flowers wreathed the ugly block-house. All the flower pots filled with blue lobelia and harebells and wherever the horse turned a cartwheel, an arch of blue clematis appeared.

"How's that for a start?" said the horse, taking a bow.

I was speechless.

"Well – have you got anything to say to me?" said the horse.

"Thank you!" I said at last.

"You're welcome," said the horse. "I'm going to have to go now. What's your name?"

"Cowslip," I said. "And that's another thing –"

The horse interrupted me with a loud, braying laugh.

"*Cowslip*?" it said. "That's a funny name."

"Yes," I said. "It is."

The horse was beginning to waver and shimmer like a heat-haze. It was growing fainter all the time. It rose in the air.

"Call when you want me," it said, its voice fading. "Just 'Blue' will do."

Then it was gone. The sound of the traffic came drifting back. And there I stood, surrounded by my beautiful blue garden.

Chapter 9

Kevin had been away. When he came back he brought us another e-mail from another place I'd never heard of. Tommy got me to read it to him twice before we went to sleep.

"Hallo, Everyone!" it said. "Having a lovely time! Saw flying fish yesterday. There's been a little mix-up with Dad's charts, but he's getting it sorted. Hope you're all well and happy. I'm off to make another lasagne for tomorrow. Dad's favourite. Love, Mum (and Dad)."

"Read it again, Cowslip," said Tommy.

"Read it yourself," I said.

I folded the e-mail into a paper dart and threw it across the chalk line, knocking over a little herd of dinosaurs.

Tommy grabbed the dart and  started grumbling to himself as he smoothed it out. I turned away and buried my head beneath my pillow. I lay there and thought about the horse.

Of course, I'd fallen asleep on the roof and had a dream. That must be it. A blue horse? Either I'd dreamed it or I was going mad. Or perhaps I'd wished so hard that I'd imagined it all. So much for wishes. I could just see myself riding into the playground on Blazing Blue. Not. I'd be a figure of fun. "Presenting – Cowslip Pike, riding her Ridiculous Horse!" I could already hear the jeers.

Yes – it was quite comforting to realise that I'd dreamed the whole thing. A blue horse? Ha! Ha! I snuggled down under my duvet and fell fast asleep.

I was woken by the sun on the bedroom ceiling. It was still very early. Tommy was fast asleep and I could hear Gran snoring in her room.

I lay there for a while, thinking about my dream. Then I got up and, still in my pyjamas, tiptoed out of the flat. I went up the flight of stairs and turned the key in the lock. I pushed at the door, but it only opened a little way; something seemed to be stopping it. I pushed harder and it burst open. A spray of blue honeysuckle swung into my face, showering me with dew.

I blinked and looked around me. The flowers were still there – if anything, there seemed to be more of them now. I walked amongst the lavender and the hyacinths and the lupins, holding my breath in case they all suddenly disappeared. But the flowers were real enough; and when I did breathe in, the scent was so incredible, it made me feel faint.

I sat with my back to the block-house. Bees

were buzzing from flower to flower and little blue butterflies fluttered against the sky. So it was real after all. I hadn't imagined it. And here was a thought – if I hadn't imagined it, the horse must be real, too.

All I had to do was call. Should I? Did I want to? Did I really want to see that strange-looking horse again? What had it said? "Just 'Blue' will do." I couldn't help myself. I stood up. I called through the blue tangles of honeysuckle:

"Blue! Blue! *Blue!*"

There was that same silence and the same fizzing in the sky. I watched and waited, and then, suddenly, there he was – Blazing Blue. He came sailing through the air and landed before me on a bed of forget-me-nots.

"I thought so!" he said. "I thought you'd want to see me again."

"The garden's still here," I said stupidly.

"Of course," said Blue. "Did you think it was going to dissolve into thin air?"

"I thought I'd dreamed it," I said.

The horse gave that sudden, braying laugh.

"So what would you like me to do for you?" he asked.

Then, as I still said nothing, he rose on its hind-legs.

"Another dance?" he asked. "Or perhaps a song —"

"No!" I said hurriedly. "No thank you."

"You'd probably like to ride me to school," said Blue. "Just to show that Venetia a thing or two."

"It's Sunday," I said, thanking my lucky stars.

"Then it's a good time for a practice," said Blue. "Come on, climb up."

He kneeled down, but I hung back.

"I don't want anyone to see us," I said.

"They won't," said the horse. "I promise."

"And I've never ridden a horse before," I said.

"It's easy," said Blue, shaking his mane. "Come along, for goodness' sake – don't shilly-shally."

And the next thing I knew, I was climbing up on his back.

Blue rose to his feet.

"Hold on to my mane," he said and he started to trot around the roof garden. I had to duck as we passed under the trellis arches and the dew spilled down on my head. I began to feel pleased with myself. There wasn't much to this riding after all, was there?

"See? You can do it," said the horse. "And now for something completely different."

And to my horror he sprang in the air and balanced on the railings. I looked down. Ugh! Once was enough. I looked away and closed my eyes.

And then I felt Blue jump. He jumped out into space.

Chapter 10

I tried to scream, but no sound came. I clung to Blue's mane, waiting for the plunge and then the Big Splat. But nothing happened and I realised that instead of going down we were going up.

"You can open your eyes now," said Blue.

We were flying! I was flying! I looked down, and there was Franklin Heights, far below us, its roof a cloud of blue.

"Would you like me to do some tricks?" said Blue.

I gave a sort of squawk, which I suppose Blue took to be a "yes", because –

"The Loop the Loop!" he announced and we performed a figure of eight in the sky.

"Now for the Vertical Zoom!" he snorted, and up we went, like a rocket.

"The Vapour Trail!" he cried; and we shot through the sky, leaving a silver-blue ribbon behind us.

We levelled out. I was shaking all over.

"Don't worry," said Blue. "Stay with me, kid – you'll be fine."

" 'Stay with me'?" I thought. "Stupid horse! Of course I'm going to stay with you."

"Where would you like to go now?" asked Blue.

I looked down. I could see the town below us, spread out like a map, the Downs on one side and the sea on the other.

"Could we have a look at my old house?" I asked.

"Sure!" said Blue. "Which one is it?"

"The yellow one," I said.

And then we were off. One moment we were looking down at the tiny yellow dot and the next we were zooming in on it, like Google Earth. The house got bigger and bigger and then, suddenly, we were landing in the front garden. Blue trotted round with me on his back, inspecting the property. I peered through the kitchen window and saw a family having breakfast at our table.

There was a boy and a girl and a baby. The boy jumped up and ran into the garden and, yes – cheek! – I'd been right! He got my bike out of the shed and started riding around. He seemed to look straight through us. It was as though we weren't there.

"He can't see us," said Blue. "Anything else?"

I could see my flower patch, full of marigolds and poppies. Someone had been watering it, then.

"No," I said.

Blue rose into the air. I had a sudden thought.

"Could we have a look at Venetia's house?" I asked.

"OK," said Blue. "It's the one with the turret, isn't it?"

Venetia's house was called Castle Towers. Well, of course it was.

"Let's look in her window," I said; and we were there, hovering outside, even before I'd finished speaking.

I peered in. So there was the famous coffin! And there was a sleeping shape under the black

duvet. As I watched, the door swung open and a woman came in. I supposed it was Sylvia, Venetia's mother.

"Come on, Venetia!" she said. "Rise and shine! You've got your extra dance class today."

The shape in the coffin sat up. Venetia's hair was rumpled and there was a scowl on her face. She was wearing a black t-shirt.

"Go away!" she snarled; and she actually threw a pillow at her mother.

Sylvia caught it. She stood her ground.

"Come along, Vee," she said. "It's a busy day. The maths tutor's coming this afternoon. Remember?"

Maths tutor? No wonder Venetia kept coming

top in maths. I'd had a vague idea that Venetia might be a vampire. Now I realised that she was something worse. She was a swot.

Venetia buried her head beneath the duvet.

"I'm staying in bed all day," she said in a muffled voice.

Her mother gave a silvery laugh.

"Oh no you're not, Vee!" she said and she snatched away the duvet.

Venetia gave a piercing scream and rolled around the bed.

"What an awful family!" said Blue. "Let's go!"

I had begun to enjoy flying. Blue seemed to have got bigger – his back was broader now. Every so often I thought I caught a glimpse of

wings flapping, but when I looked down, I saw that I was wrong.

"I think that's enough for today," said Blue and we headed for Franklin Heights. But I found that Blue was easily distracted.

"Aha! A plane!" he said.

I looked up and there, high above us, was a jet. It was climbing fast, taking off from Gatwick.

"Watch this!" said Blue, and he was off, like a dog chasing a bone.

We screamed through the sky until we were flying level with the plane – so close that I could see people through the windows. Some of them had their eyes shut, some were reading and others were peering down at the coast.

"Don't worry, they can't see us," said Blue.

But even as he spoke I saw a little girl staring at us. She turned and pulled at her mother's arm and pointed. Her mother looked straight through us and then she laughed and tickled the girl under the chin.

"That's enough of that!" said Blue suddenly and we set off at such a lick that the plane was left standing. We wheeled round over the sea and came curving in towards Franklin Heights, leaving a white vapour trail behind us.

"Home again!" said Blue, as we touched down on the roof. "How was that, then?"

I slithered down and landed on blue moss. My legs felt shaky.

"All right," I said.

"All right?" said Blue. "Just all right?"

"I quite liked the flying," I said reluctantly.

Quite honestly, seeing our house again had upset me. And as for Venetia —

"She does extra maths!" I cried.

The horse was beginning to fade.

"And that makes you jealous, does it?" he asked as his body wavered in front of me.

"Well —" I began; but Blue had gone. He'd

faded into thin air. All I could hear was his braying laugh.

Then that, too, was gone and I heard the sound of church bells from somewhere far below me. And there was another sound, too. It made me freeze. Someone was rattling at the blockhouse door.

I waited. Thank goodness I'd locked it behind me. I heard the catflap clatter backwards and forwards. Then it stopped and I heard footsteps retreating down the steps.

I waited for a long time until the coast was clear. While I waited I picked a big bunch of blue flowers. I thought they'd look nice in the living-room. I tip-toed out, locking the door behind me. But as I slipped the key into my pocket there was a loud "Pop!" like a balloon bursting and my flowers vanished. I was left holding a handful of air.

POP!

chapter 11

Here's another week from my diary. Well – if I can have an imaginary horse, I can have an imaginary diary, can't I?

MONDAY: Alice comes up to me in playground. Says, "Come on, Moo. You made the horse up, didn't you?" I say, "I _have_ got a horse." Alice frowns. Says "What's got into you? I don't want to be friends with someone who tells porkies." She runs off to join Venetia, who's telling everyone about her new trampoline.

TUESDAY: Miss Grant says that today's P.E. is going to be Music and Movement and that we're doing it in the playground. Turns on the cassette player. Says, "This *is the dance of the Dying Swan from Swan Lake. Express yourselves."*

To be continued: (Too much to tell you in a small diary.)

We started to move around. I'd no idea what a dying swan felt like so I tried moving from side to side and looking sad. It fitted in with the way I was feeling, anyhow. Some of the boys started galloping round me, making whinnying noises. Micky Grimshaw said, "We're being dying *horses.*"

I ignored them. The others were whirling about, flapping their arms. They all looked pretty silly. Suddenly Venetia Best came leaping out into the middle of the playground. She did a pirouette and started to dance around, pointing her toes. She had a soulful look on her face. She fluttered her arms and stood on one leg. Slowly everyone else stopped dancing and formed a circle round her. Some of them even began to clap.

It was almost more than I could bear. Without thinking I raised my eyes skywards and whispered:

"Oh, *Blue!*"

And that was my mistake.

Fizz! went the sky and the sound of the music faded and there was my horse, standing before me on his hind legs. He looked much smaller than usual — about the size of your average sheep. His mane had grown and his eyelashes were twice their usual length. He fluttered them at me and said:

"Watch this!"

And he started to dance along behind Venetia.
I sneaked a glance around; to my relief, no-one
seemed to have noticed him.

Every time Venetia leaped in the air, so did
Blue. But whereas Venetia jumped elegantly,
Blue jumped like a clown. He whirled round and

fell on his bottom; then he jumped up and did a
somersault. Still no-one seemed to notice him;
they were all riveted by Venetia's performance.

"Come on," said Blue, dancing up to me with
a silly look on his face. "Don't let her hog the
limelight. Follow me."

And I did. I don't know why. I wish now I hadn't. I jumped around behind Blue, who was following Venetia. I knew I looked like an idiot but I didn't care. I heard gasps but I took no notice. All of a sudden, Blue leaped towards Venetia. I did the same. But whereas Blue sailed right through Venetia and out the other side, I didn't. I collided with her and we both went sprawling. I could hear Blue's laugh as he faded into the sky.

At first, there was just silence.

I sat up.

"Well, we're both *dead* swans now," I said.

Still no-one said anything.

Then – would you believe it? – there was a chorus of boos.

And they were directed at me – *me!* Miss Grant was bending over Venetia who was moaning that she'd hurt her knee.

"Cowslip!" she said. "Why did you *do* that?

We were all enjoying Venetia's dance. That was very spiteful. I'm sending you to the Head."
Now back to my diary.

TUESDAY (CONTINUED): The Head gives me a bad behaviour mark. Says I must apologize to Venetia. Marches me to the office, where Venetia is having a plaster put on her knee. Stands over me while I say sorry. Venetia smirks. Probably the worst day of my life so far.

Venetia's knee

WEDNESDAY: Venetia makes remarkable recovery. Alice says, "Moo! What did you think you were doing yesterday? You ruined Venetia's dance. And you were laughing and talking to yourself all the time. Have you gone mad?"

THURSDAY: Venetia extra nasty to me. Says, "Where do you keep this horse of yours, then?" I say, "In stables."

Venetia says, "Which stables?" and I say, "None of your business." Venetia says, "You mean it's a pretend stables – like your pretend horse." All the others laugh.

FRIDAY: The school Disco. Oh hooray. I am not just a cowslip, I am a wallflower. Sit and watch the others dance. Even my brother seems to be having a nice time. He and his little friends push each other over at the back of the Hall and roll around on the floor.

Venetia has invented a new dance. It's a line dance and all her best friends (i.e. most of the class) are in it. It's a bit like a Mexican Wave with clever footwork. Brian Big Ears gives me snidey look and tags on to end of line.

Thank goodness that's over. We're back home. Gran is watching T.V. It's the news. Suddenly she gasps and drops the photo of Bobby Six. What's up?

chapter 12

I heard the newsreader say something about "yacht" and "the Indian Ocean".

"What is it?" I asked.

"Ssh!" said Gran.

The newsreader was still speaking.

"An intensive air and sea search is under way," she said, "for the yacht the *Mary Ellen*, which disappeared three days ago in the Indian Ocean. No radio contact has been made."

"What!" I cried.

"What?" asked Tommy, poking his head round the door.

"It's your Mum and Dad's boat!" said Gran. "Oh no! First Bobby Six and now this!"

"What's happened?" asked Tommy.

"The *Mary Ellen's* disappeared," I said.

Tommy stood there, his mouth open. He'd turned pale. I felt frozen. I didn't know what to do – I just stood there, like Tommy, rooted to the spot.

We watched every news programme we could find that evening. The *Mary Ellen* was on all of them – but the news didn't change; the *Mary Ellen* seemed to have disappeared into thin air.

"I suppose no news is good news," said Gran.

And that's when the phone started to ring – neighbours and friends at first, wanting to know what was going on and then the local radio station. I couldn't bear it. I made up a friend called Lydia who lived three floors down and told Gran I was going to see her.

"All right, dear," said Gran, still on the phone.

I tip-toed out and went straight up to the roof garden.

Although it was late, the sky was still blue; over the sea the sun was dipping towards the horizon.

"Blue!" I shouted. "*Blue!*"

It wasn't an invitation, either – it was an order. All the fright I was feeling came boiling out of me like rage. I even stamped my foot.

"*Blue!*" I yelled again.

A faint-looking Blue appeared out of the fading sky.

"Yes, Cow?" he said, landing in front of me.

"*Cowslip!*" I yelled, stamping my foot again.

"What's the matter?" asked Blue. "You look

a bit put out."

Somehow or other I couldn't bring myself to say the words.

What I wanted to say was "Mum and Dad are missing," but I couldn't. Instead I shouted:

"You stupid horse!"

"Manners!" said Blue. "What exactly am I meant to have done?"

"You *know* what you've done!" I raged. "Got me into trouble at school. Made a fool of me. I got a black mark – all because of your stupid dancing."

"Oh – that," said Blue. "But you wanted to upstage Venetia, didn't you?"

"Not like that!" I said, stamping my foot again. "I got booed. And I had to apologize to her."

"Well – you *did* hurt her, didn't you?" said the

horse, idly chomping on a strand of morning glory. I noticed he looked different – he'd grown bigger again and his mane and tail were threaded with forget-me-nots. He was wearing a wreath of blue roses on his head, which tipped down over one eye.

"Aargh!" I yelled, jumping up and down.

"You're a very ungrateful girl," said Blue. "Look at all the nice things I've done for you recently."

I was so angry I wasn't listening.

"You're not even a proper horse!" I screamed.

"No?" said Blue. "I thought I was what you wanted."

I let that pass.

"You're ridiculous!" I fumed. "You look stupid. I'm glad no-one can see you. I'd be ashamed to be seen out with you."

"Then that's easily settled," said Blue. "Just

don't call me any more."

As he spoke, the sun slipped into the sea.

"Bye-bye," said Blue; and that was it — he was gone. I was left there on the roof, the blue flowers nodding around me, while a silver moon like a fingernail began to climb the sky.

chapter 13

On Saturday morning the TV crew arrived. Gran sat there on the sofa while they filmed; they arranged me and Tommy on either side of her. Tommy was holding a brontosaurus and Gran held two photos – one of Mum and Dad and one of Bobby Six. I just sat there, feeling grumpy, while they asked us questions – how long had Mum and Dad been gone? How come they were crewing? Had Dad passed all his navigation exams?

"You must miss them a lot," said the interviewer.

"Yes," whispered Tommy, sniffing.

It was awful. I felt crosser than ever. I hadn't

said anything yet.

Suddenly the camera zoomed in on me and the interviewer shoved a microphone into my face.

"And how do *you* feel, Cowslip?" she asked.

That was the last straw.

"How do you *think* I feel?" I yelled, jumping to my feet.

I stumbled out of the room. Behind me I heard someone say: "Cut! We'll go on without her. We'll start again. Now then, Mrs Pike, what exactly were your son and daughter-in-law doing in the Indian Ocean?"

Up on the roof it was hotter than ever. The sky was very blue – blazing blue. I didn't call him. I knew he wouldn't come. The flowers had begun to droop in the heat. I sank down on the blue moss. What a disaster! What was going to happen now? All sorts of thoughts crowded into my mind but I pushed them away.

I tried watering some of the flowers but it didn't make any difference; they seemed to droop even more.

That evening we watched the local news. It started off with a shot of all three of us on the sofa; I was scowling like mad. Then it cut to Gran and Tommy. Tommy was snuffling and chewing the tail of his brontosaurus. The interview finished with the camera zooming in on Gran's photos.

"He was a lovely bird," said Gran. "So friendly. Always so cheerful. The best friend I ever had."

The weekend was so awful, I was almost pleased to be back at school. And things were different; people had seen the news. Miss Grant sent me out to take the register to the office. I lurked outside the door and listened.

"You've probably all heard that Cowslip's had some really bad news," she said. "She and her brother must be very worried. Try and be extra nice to her today."

Huh! I stomped off down the corridor. They need not think they could get round me that easily. Especially as they'd all been so nasty to me last week. I'd show them.

The only good thing about all this was that everyone stopped calling me "Poo". At break time some of them came up and said they were sorry; others just looked at me in a pitying way.

Venetia sidled up and said:

"What'll happen if they don't come back? I suppose you'll have to live with your Gran forever."

And then she pretended to look really, really sorry.

"I wonder what's happened to them, Cow?"

said Micky Grimshaw. "Do you think they've been kidnapped by pirates?"

"Or perhaps they've sunk," said Alex Johnson.

"And been eaten by a whale," said Luke Turner. "A whale with great big sharp teeth –"

"Stop it!" said Alice, stepping forward and putting her arm round me. "That's not very nice. Do you want to talk about it, Moo?"

I shook her off.

"No!" I said. "Just leave me alone."

I ran away across the playing field. The brown grass crackled beneath my feet and the sun beat down on my head but I didn't care. I just wanted to get away from them all. Alice followed me. She caught up with me in a corner of the field.

"I know you're a bit blue, Moo," she said, touching my arm.

I shook her off again. She'd used the wrong word.

"Blue?" I growled. "What do you mean?"

"Well, sad," said Alice. "I only said 'blue' because you kept talking about being blue the other day – you know, when you pushed Venetia over. You *are* blue, aren't you?"

"Blue?" I shrieked. "*Blue?*"

Alice jumped back, looking worried.

There was that fizzing above me and the shouts from the playground faded away. There before me stood Blazing Blue, pawing the dry grass and shaking his mane.

"Well?" he said. "Is there something you want to say to me?"

I gulped.

"I'm sorry, Blue," I said. "I didn't mean it."

"Apology accepted," said Blue. "I knew you didn't mean it. I'm really a fine-looking horse."

He shook his head and capered about. I noticed that he seemed to have grown even more and that his mane and tail were woven into hundreds of plaits. There was a big blue bow on his head.

I gave a deep sigh and then it all came tumbling out. My parents – the yacht – the TV crew. I went on and on.

"You poor thing," said Blue and I realised tears were running down my face. "There, there!" he added.

He nuzzled me; then – Yuk! – he started licking the tears off my cheeks.

"OK! OK!" I said, backing away. I wiped my face with my hand. "Blue – help me! Please! Find Mum and Dad for me."

"No can do, I'm afraid," said Blue. "The Indian Ocean's way out of my range. Don't worry, Cow. No news –"

"Cowslip!" I said.

"Sorry!" he said. "Don't worry, Cowslip. No news is good news, you know."

That's just what Gran had said.

"You're not being much help," I muttered; but Blue was already fading away. Through his shimmering body I could see Alice, haring off as fast as she could towards the school.

They took me to the office and sat me in the armchair. Alice had told them I'd been crying and talking to myself – saying I was sorry and all sorts of other things. They let me stay there till lunchtime; it was nice not to have to do maths. I closed my eyes and thought about Mum and Dad.

All the same, I was really pleased when they let me out. I couldn't believe how hungry I was. It must have been all that crying. I fell on my lunch-box and gobbled everything up in double-quick time.

"Pleased to see you're feeling better, Moo," said Micky Grimshaw.

Then they all seemed to forget about me and started talking about pirates.

chapter 14

The days dragged on. Each of them seemed to last a fortnight. It was awful. Here's some more from my diary, so you can see for yourselves how awful it was.

THE REST OF MONDAY: Gran spends most of evening on telephone. "I know! I know! It's been six days now. Still — no news is good news," etc, etc.

Tread on spiky pterodactyl getting into bed. Scream at Tommy and throw it at him. One of the wings breaks off. Tommy cries.

TUESDAY: Everyone playing pirates in playground, except for Luke Turner, who is a gigantic whale. Runs around with mouth open, barging people over.

Thank goodness for roof garden.
Flowers have perked up again. Let
Blue do ballet dance for me. Still no news.

WEDNESDAY: Feel really low. I hate school. Venetia
getting up my nose (as usual).
News at last. "The search in the Indian Ocean for the
missing yacht, the Mary Ellen, has been abandoned. Hope
is fading ..." etc, etc. Blue and Gran were right, then.
No news is good news.

Call Blue. He offers to sing lullaby.
"It will help you sleep." Feel so bad, let
him. Feel worse than ever. Lie awake
half the night.

THURSDAY: All the kids playing shipwrecks. Hear
Venetia asking Alice, Lizzie and Tara to a sleep-over.
Says, "Six o'clock sharp. Don't be late. We're having purple
food." Yuk! Still no news. Just falling asleep when Tommy

says, "Do you think Mum and Dad will come back, Cowslip?" I say, "Don't know. Why're you asking me?" Turn my back on him.

FRIDAY: Hottest day yet. After school go to roof garden and call Blue. Ask him to take me for ride. We go to Venetia's turret and hover around outside. Venetia sitting in coffin. Alice and others on sleeping bags on floor. All eating purple spaghetti. Venetia says, "It's purple yoghourt next. Yummy!" Alice clutches stomach. Says, "I feel sick!" and throws up over Venetia's duvet. It's purple. Venetia screams at her. "You're disgusting! Get out!" Alice leaves, looking pale. Venetia says, "Either of you two not appreciate adventurous cooking?" They look scared and shake heads. I ask Blue to take me home.

Back on roof garden a horrible shock in store for me.

chapter 15

A splash of red stood out against a cloud of lobelia. It looked so strange against all that blue that I went to investigate.

I stared. I couldn't believe my eyes. It was a red stegosaurus, standing on the rim of a pot. Thump! went my heart and it missed a beat. How had it got there? Tommy? Had I left the door open? I tried it, but no, it was firmly locked. I forgot all about Blue, who had faded away behind me.

I picked up the stegosaurus and stared at it. It could only be Tommy's. And then I had an idea. The cat flap! Tommy must have thrown the dinosaur through. Perhaps it was him I'd heard banging at it the other day.

I wandered around the roof garden, looking at the small creature in my hand, and working things out. I rounded the block-house and – horrors! – there was another one. This one was a brontosaurus. Tommy could never have thrown it here. It balanced in a pot of lupins – and higher up, on the parapet, were two more. An electric shock seemed to jolt through my body.

It was then that I knew. I knew for sure that Tommy had got into my garden. And the way he'd got in was through the cat flap. There was just enough room for a very small boy to wriggle through. I felt the blood pumping in my ears.

I raced back into the flat. In the bedroom Tommy had arranged some of his dinosaurs in a model boat and was pushing them across the floor.

"You've been in my garden!" I ground out, hardly able to speak.

Tommy looked up.

"Get back, Cowslip," he said. "You've stepped over my line."

That did it. I kicked his boatload of dinosaurs so that they went flying round the room. Then I rubbed out the chalk line with my foot.

"Stop it! Stop it!" cried Tommy.

I bent down and shoved my face into his. I must have been a frightening sight, because Tommy began to scream.

"Tell me the truth!" I hissed, grabbing his t-shirt. "You've been out there, haven't you?"

"Where?" screamed Tommy.

"On my garden!" I cried. "Don't lie! You've left your beastly little dinosaurs lying around all over the place."

"It's not just *your* garden," sniffled

Tommy.

I shook him.

"Tell me what you saw!" I yelled.

"Nothing!" screamed Tommy. "What do you mean, Cowslip?"

"Tell me!" I yelled again. "What did you see?"

"Just chimneys and old flowerpots," sobbed Tommy. "That's all."

Gran came rushing in.

"What's all this screaming?" she said. "Cowslip! What are you doing? Let go of Tommy at once."

I loosened my grip on Tommy's t-shirt.

"What's happened to you, Cowslip?" asked Gran. "You seem to be turning into a horrible bully. I'm surprised at you. Come out to the other room and leave your brother alone."

She grabbed my arm and hauled me after her.

Tommy rubbed his face on his sleeve and started to collect up his dinosaurs.

"I hate you, Cowslip," he muttered. "I really, *really* hate you."

I *did* feel sorry for what I'd done. But the thought of Tommy, up there, on my secret garden, had been too much. I fell asleep that night deciding to be nicer to my little brother in future and to fix the cat-flap so that he couldn't get through.

But my good resolutions came to nothing. Because when I woke up the next morning, Tommy had gone.

chapter 16

Tommy's pyjamas were neatly folded on his bed. His clothes were gone and a lot of his dinosaurs seemed to be missing. In the kitchen some chocolate fingers had disappeared from the biscuit barrel and there was one less can of coke in the fridge.

There was a note on the work surface. It said, "Gon to find mum and dad."

"He can't have got far," said Gran. "He's probably down with Mrs Everett. I'll go and look."

While she was gone I sneaked a quick look around the roof. There was no sign of Tommy. But something strange was happening. A shadow

passed over the garden. And when
I looked up, there was a cloud – the
first cloud I'd seen for weeks. It floated on and
although the air was hot, I started to shiver. I met
Gran as she came puffing up the stairs. "He's not
there," she said. "We'll have to look outside."

We went down in the lift and started searching.
Bert the caretaker said he'd take a look in the
basement. He came back, covered in cobwebs.

"Not a sausage," he said.

We rushed around the streets, asking if anyone
had seen a small, fair-haired boy. But no-one
had – it was as though Tommy had disappeared
into thin air. Every so often I caught sight of
Bobby Six staring down at me from a tattered
poster.

"We'll make some phone calls," said Gran.
"I'll try his friends."

Gran rang half a dozen numbers, but each
time she drew a blank.

"That's it," said Gran. "We'll have to call the police."

"First my budgie – then my son and daughter-in-law – now this!" sniffed Gran.

"Your brother must have been missing his Mum and Dad," said the police constable, taking me to one side.

Must he? I hadn't really noticed.

"Don't know," I said.

"Did he ever talk to you about them?" she asked.

Suddenly I felt awful. He'd tried, hadn't he? And I'd told him to shut up. Were they going to arrest me?

"Did he?" she repeated.

"Not really," I said.

"Your Gran said you and Tommy had a row last night," said the police constable.

I grunted.

"Can you tell me what it was about?" she asked.

I was silent.

"Cowslip?" she said.

"Nothing much," I muttered. I couldn't tell them about the roof garden, could I?

The police searched the flat, just in case Tommy was hiding under a bed or had locked himself into a cupboard. The other police constable looked out into the corridor.

"Where does that go?" he asked, jerking his head in the direction of the roof garden door.

"Onto the roof," said Gran. "But it's been locked for years and the key's missing."

The police constable went up the steps and pushed at the door, but it didn't budge. He ignored the cat-flap. I suppose he had no idea just how small Tommy was.

"Now – don't go out again, Mrs Pike," he said to Gran. "Stay here, in case he comes back. We'll be in touch."

Then they left. They took Tommy's note with them and a photo of a happy, smiling Tommy, taken on his birthday last year. I realised he hadn't looked like that for ages.

Gran sank into her armchair. It wasn't long before she was asleep and snoring. I tip-toed out and went up to the roof-garden. I wanted to talk to Blue. I was sure he could find Tommy for me.

I called and called but he didn't come. And then I realised why. All day long the cloud had been building up. That little white cloud I'd seen earlier had turned into one dark mass that covered the sky. There wasn't a patch of blue to be seen. My flowers had already begun to droop.

I stood there, feeling desperate and guilty. And as I stood there, the first fat drops of rain began to fall.

Chapter 17

That night the heat was terrible. I could hear thunder in the distance and rain pattering against the window. I rolled around, feeling hot and sticky; and when I finally managed to fall asleep, I had a dream. Well, a nightmare, really.

I dreamed Blue and I were flying through the sky. He was messing about – doing aerobatics and flying backwards. He also kept changing into ridiculous shapes – first a pig, then a goat and now he was pretending to be a dolphin. I got crosser and crosser. I knew there was somewhere I needed to be, but I couldn't quite remember where.

Suddenly we dropped like a stone and landed

in front of a cave.

"He's down there," said Blue as I slid off his back. He turned a cartwheel. "You'll have to go after him."

"Come with me," I said.

"I can't," said Blue. He did a back flip. "I'm a day-time horse, remember. A blue skies horse." He faded away and his voice came whispering out of nowhere. "You're on your own."

The cave was dark and damp. I felt my way along the walls, brushing away the cobwebs that drifted into my face. Suddenly the ground beneath me gave way and I found myself whizzing downwards on a sort of helter-skelter.

Bump! I landed on a cushion of orange moss. Above me the sky was orange, too. Flocks of pterodactyls glided across it.

I picked myself up and started walking. On either side of me, awful roars shook the frond forest. A herd of chicken-sized dinosaurs

ran across my path and disappeared into the undergrowth, making a sort of twittering sound. I pressed on. In front of me I saw an enormous coffin. I watched as the lid swung back and a dinosaur sprang out like a jack-in-the-box. It had spines down its back and a ruff round its neck and the face of Venetia Best. It rushed towards me.

"Yo! Venetia!" I said.

"Poo!" said the dinosaur and roared.

So I roared back. And the amazing thing was

that the Venetia creature just dwindled away like a pricked balloon until all that was left was its wide, roaring mouth – and then that was gone, too.

I plodded on, following a trail of plastic dinosaurs. At last I found him. I found Tommy. He was curled up, fast asleep, under a giant fern tree.

"Tommy!" I shouted and he woke up.

"Go away, Cowslip!" he mumbled.

I was taken aback.

"I've come to rescue you," I said.

"I don't need rescuing," said Tommy. "I like it here. I'm staying with the dinosaurs. They're my friends."

"But we've all been looking for you," I said. "Please come home, Tommy."

"No!" said my brother. "I don't want to. I don't like you any more, Cowslip."

I grabbed his arm and started tugging.

Tommy fought back. As we struggled, dinosaurs crept from the undergrowth and formed a circle round us; I noticed they were clapping Tommy and booing me.

And then there was a blinding flash and one gigantic roar and on the horizon a volcano exploded. Molten lava and tons of rock came hurtling towards us. Tommy slipped from my grasp. I woke with a start. I was bathed in sweat. The room shook with another crash – and this one was right overhead.

The thunderstorm raged about over Franklin Heights. The lightning flashes lit Tommy's empty bed and I thought of him out there, alone in the storm. I counted the time between the flashes and bangs until I reached twenty; then I fell asleep. And outside the rain poured down as though it would never stop.

chapter 18

When morning came it was still raining. Gran boiled me an egg but I couldn't eat anything. After a while the police arrived.

"We're concentrating on the marina," they said. "We think that's the most likely place – he may well have stowed away on a boat."

They asked a few more questions then they went off again.

"Try not to worry," said the police constable over her shoulder. "No news is good news."

"There's nothing we can do," said Gran. "We'll just have to sit and wait."

Gran found waiting easier than me. She sank

into her armchair and dropped off. I prowled around the flat, peering out at the rain. The thunder was still rumbling overhead. I couldn't bear it.

I tip-toed out and went up to the roof garden. The door had swollen with the rain and I had to charge at it with my shoulder several times before it would budge.

My flowers lay on the ground, beaten down by the storm. Everything was ruined. I stood there, listening to the pitter-patter of the rain as it splashed into the puddles. Above me dark clouds swilled around.

"Blue!" I cried; but nothing happened. All I heard was the growling of the thunder. I looked towards the sea – the Downs – the river; somewhere, out there, was Tommy. But where? I'd got to find him.

I searched the sky – and suddenly, above me, I saw a chink in the clouds. A tiny patch of blue, as big as my hand, had opened up. This was it. It was my last chance.

"Blue!" I yelled. I had to shout above the thunder.

Nothing happened. The patch of blue was getting smaller all the time. I was desperate. I gathered up all my strength.

"BLUE –UE –UE!"
I screamed.

And then
it happened.
Something

started to happen with that patch of blue. There was a wobbling – a wriggling – as though something was trying to get through. And then – yes! – there was Blue! He struggled out as the hole in the clouds closed up behind him and flopped down towards me.

He looked as though he'd been squeezed out of a tube of toothpaste. He was very long and thin, like a sausage dog. He lay there, panting, unable to speak, while around us the rain danced in the puddles.

"Blue!" I said and I stroked his mane. "You're here!"

At last Blue spoke.

"You called?" he said in a faint voice.

"Tommy's run away!" I said. "Please help me find him."

Blue struggled to his feet.

"You seem a very *unfortunate* girl," he said. "First the budgerigar, then your parents, now this." He sounded just like Gran. "Why's he run away?"

I was silent.

"Cowslip?" said Blue.

"It was my fault!" I burst out at last. "I was horrible to him. I bullied him. I drove him away. He's gone to find Mum and Dad. The police think he's gone to the marina."

Blue sighed.

"Let's see what we can do, then," he said and his whole frame quivered.

I climbed onto his long, thin body and Blue braced himself.

"I warn you, Cowslip," he said. "I don't know if I've got the strength for this. Getting through the clouds has worn me out."

"Please try, Blue!" I said as he struggled up onto the railings.

Then he jumped. I could see his hooves flailing the air.

"It's no good – I can't get any height," said Blue and we floated down until we landed in the street outside the flats.

Blue shook himself, as though to buck himself up. Then he started to sniff the ground like a bloodhound.

"He went this way!" he said suddenly.

And we were off. We raced through the streets, Blue with his nose to the ground. The rain was easing off now. Blue went on sniffing. We passed little groups of people; I even spotted some kids from school, but no-one saw us. I realised we weren't heading for the marina at all. We were going in the opposite direction.

"He went in here," said Blue, stopping at a terraced house.

He jumped the gate and started sniffing around the garden.

"Wait there," I said and slid off. "I'll go and ask."

I knocked on the door. After a while an old lady appeared, leaning heavily on a stick.

"Excuse me!" I said. "Have you seen my

brother, Tommy? He's about this high with fair hair. We think he came in here."

" 'We'?" said the old lady, looking around.

"Well, *me*," I said. "I think he came in here. Is he indoors with you?"

"No he's not," said the old lady. "But I think I know the boy you mean. I spotted him yesterday – the little blighter!"

Yes! A result!

"He's stolen my plastic bath," said the old lady. "It was hanging there – on the wall. I saw him out of the window. He was walking off with it over his head. I couldn't do anything about it – I'm too slow on my feet."

A plastic bath?

"Which way did he go?" I asked.

"That way!" said the old lady. And my blood ran cold; because she pointed towards the river.

chapter 19

"She's right!" said Blue as we snuffled along the street towards the river. "He definitely went this way."

When we got to the river bank Blue went sniffing through the grass around the picnic area. I knew this place well, because we used to come here a lot with Mum and Dad.

Suddenly Blue plunged into a footpath through the undergrowth and I knew – I just knew – where we were going. Tommy and I used to play here sometimes. Blue stopped before a cave. It wasn't really a cave – not like the one in my dream – it was more of a hollow that kids had scooped out in the sandstone. It only went back a metre or so.

My heart sank. It was empty. But – hang on!

"Look!" I cried, jumping down. "A coke can! Biscuit wrappers! Blue – these are the ones he took from the kitchen. He must have stayed the night here."

"A very untidy boy," said Blue. "It's boys like him who give children a bad name."

Then he started sniffing around like mad.

"Hold onto my tail," he said. "I know which way he went."

Then we were off, pushing through the undergrowth, ducking under branches and stepping over brambles. Suddenly the ground gave way beneath us.

"Whoa!" cried Blue.

We were sliding down a sandy slope – out of the bushes and down towards the river.

We ended up on a little sandy shore. The

water was high because of all the rain and the river was running fast to the sea. My heart missed a beat. There on the sand were the marks of something – a plastic bath? – that had been dragged towards the water. And then I saw the clincher. Right by the water's edge lay a toy dinosaur. A diplodocus.

"He went in here," said Blue. "Not long ago."

I was frantic.

"Quick! Let's get air-sea rescue!" I said, tugging at Blue's tail.

"No time," said Blue.

"But you're not strong enough, are you?" I said in despair.

"Wait!" said Blue.

He drew a deep breath and shivered all over. Suddenly there was a twanging sound and he snapped back into shape like a piece of elastic.

"Jump up!" he panted.

I did as he said and Blue took another deep breath. Then he jumped. Splash! We landed in the muddy water.

"Hold on!" snorted Blue as he struggled back to the bank. "We'll try again."

This time he did it. He leaped – and he flew! We skimmed the water, heading down-river. I examined the river banks as we went. No sign of Tommy. Where could he be? Soon we reached the river mouth and the open sea. The water was dark and rough. Surely Tommy couldn't be out there?

"I've got to go higher," said Blue.

The skies were clearing. A ray of sunshine fell on the sea. "There!" said Blue.

I peered, but I couldn't see anything.

"Over there," said Blue, pointing his hoof.

And this time I did see him – a tiny dot in the middle of the waves. We drew closer and closer and I could see him clearly. Tommy was kneeling in the bath, trying to paddle with a small plank of wood.

We streaked down and landed next to him. I had to keep blinking the salt spray out of my eyes.

The bath was half-full of water. It was strange, though. Tommy didn't look frightened. He kept his eyes on the horizon and kept on paddling.

"Tommy!" I screamed. "You idiot!"

Tommy just stared straight ahead.

"He can't hear you," said Blue.

At that moment a giant wave crashed into

the bath and flipped it over. Tommy was left floundering in the water.

"Quick!" said Blue. "Grab him!"

I leaned over and caught hold of Tommy's jacket. I pulled him onto Blue's back and sat him in front of me. He didn't move. He just lay there with his eyes closed.

"Blue!" I screamed. "Tommy's dead!"

"No he's not," said Blue, who was struggling to rise into the air like an injured duck. "Look again."

I did and I saw that Tommy was sleeping. Yes – he was fast asleep. He even began to snore. And while I was looking at Tommy and watching the rise and fall of his chest, Blue rose in the air.

We flew over the sea and then over the land; and I held Tommy tight, all the way back to Franklin Heights.

chapter 20

Blue kept puffing and blowing; he found the journey really hard. On the roof garden he flopped to his knees and Tommy and I rolled off. Tommy was still half-asleep; I struggled to pull him to his feet. I could hear Blue mumbling something behind me.

"… used it all up," he was saying.

"All what?" I asked, trying to lift Tommy and not really concentrating.

"My strength," said Blue. "My Blueness."

I was half-carrying, half-dragging Tommy to the door.

"I may not see you again," I heard Blue say.

What? I looked round. But he was already

fading fast. And as Blue disappeared, the last of my flowers disappeared, too. "Blue!" I cried, but he was gone. There was nothing I could do.

I unlocked the door, dragged Tommy through and locked it again. I was just wondering how we were going to get down the stairs when Tommy opened his eyes.

"Where am I?" he asked.

"It's all right, Tommy," I said. "You're at Gran's. Can you walk?"

"Fink so," he said and we staggered down the stairs together and along the corridor.

Gran shot to her feet as we came through the door.

"Tommy!" she cried. "Where have you been?"

"Don't know," said Tommy, rubbing his eyes.

"Cowslip?" said Gran.

"I found him in the corridor," I said, telling a little white lie.

Luckily Gran believed me.

"Look at you, Tommy!" she cried. "You're soaking wet! Come on – let's get you changed."

Later on, the police arrived. They questioned me and Tommy, and I stuck to my story. Tommy had begun to remember things, though.

"I went to find Mum and Dad," he said.

"Where did you go?" asked the policewoman.

"I went down the river," said Tommy. "In a boat. And then I sailed over the sea."

"Did you?" said the policewoman. "And then what happened?"

Tommy blinked.

"Don't know," he said. "I can't remember. Fink I went to sleep.

"Perhaps it was a dream," said the policewoman.

Tommy blinked again.

"Dunno," he said.

"He must have slept outside somewhere," said the policewoman to Gran as she was showing them out. "I don't suppose we'll ever know. And as for going to sea in a boat – well, he must have dreamed it, mustn't he?"

"Or made it up," said Gran.

And that was that. Except – that evening something else happened. Something wonderful. And this time Blue had nothing to do with it.

"Brr! Brr!"

"Get the phone, will you, Cowslip?" said Gran, who was heating up some spaghetti hoops in the kitchen.

"COWSLIP!" It was Mrs Everett, screaming down the phone. "Put the TV on – NOW!"

It was the news. The whole screen was filled with a picture of the *Mary Ellen*.

"Now for the story of an amazing sea rescue," said the announcer. "After being given up for lost for the last two weeks, the entire crew of the *Mary Ellen* has been found alive and well in the Indian Ocean."

Yippee! Tommy and I jumped around and Gran sank down in her chair. The *Mary Ellen* had run aground on a coral reef. It was miles away from where the search had been taking place; it was only by chance that they'd been spotted by a passing fishing boat. So it was all a bit of a mystery.

"Everyone on board is safe and well," said the announcer. "We'll bring you more news as it comes in."

Tommy and I hugged each other and Gran hugged us both.

"Thank goodness!" said Gran. "Oh my goodness!"

And she rushed out to the kitchen as the smell of burning spaghetti filled the flat.

chapter 21

Hooray! The last week of term! And here's the last entry from my diary. (Almost.)

MONDAY: TV before breakfast. Picture of Mum and Dad. Big News story breaking. Mr Lowe, (millionaire), refusing to pay their fare home. Why?

At school, everyone nice. Alec Johnson says, "Your Mum and Dad are famous now, Cowslip." Yes. But what for, exactly? Alice runs up. Hugs me. Says, "I'm sorry for everything, Moo. I hate Venetia. She made me eat purple food. I was sick." I say, "I know". Alice puzzled. "How?" I just laugh.

TUESDAY: More news. Screen filled with red face of Mr Lowe. Raging about "terrible navigation" and "awful cooking". Cheek! Mutters something about "accident with radio equipment." Roars "They need not think they're getting any more out of me!"

At school, Venetia says "So! Poo! Your Dad can't steer and your Mum can't cook!" I say nothing. Smile, which really annoys Venetia. Keep thinking of dinosaur face and pricked balloon.

Evening news. Mum and Dad interviewed. Dad says the boo-boo with the navigation was "a mistake anyone could make. I mistook north for south. Easily done." Mum chimes in, "And if Mr Lowe hadn't thrown my lasagne and smashed the radio equipment we'd have been found in no time."

Turns out a TV company are going to fly Mum and Dad home in return for an 'exclusive'.

WEDNESDAY: Sports Day. Venetia gets a trophy for winning high jump, long jump and the egg and spoon race. Waves trophy about and says, "And you're all welcome to come and see me get another at the Horse Show. It's on Saturday." Huh!

Later on, up to roof garden. No flowers. Empty pots. Sky blue again. Try calling Blue but he doesn't show. Suppose I've worn him out with all those calls for help. Would like to say thank you, though.

Play dinosaurs with Tommy. Tommy says, "Cowslip – were you riding a horse?" Me: "No." Tommy: "Oh. I thought you were."

THURSDAY: Good day at school. Our teacher reads out a poem I've written. It starts "Blue, Blue, I really miss you." Venetia sniggers. Says "Oh – is this your imaginary horse, Poo?" I smile and look away. She looks annoyed.

After school, Mum and Dad come home. Hooray! Film cameras follow them in. Point them at us jumping around and hugging. Then Mrs Everett and Kenny and a lot of Mum and Dad's friends come round and we have a big party. It's brilliant.

Put telly on. Mr Lowe, saying, "It was lasagne, lasagne, lasagne. Chick-pea lasagne. I'd had enough."

Everyone laughs. Mum says, "You liked it, though, didn't you, Dave?" Dad says, "It was lovely, babe." And he gives her a hug. Says, "Yachting's not all it's cracked up to be. East, West, home's best." Someone says, "Oh – you know your East from your West, then, Dave?" and everyone doubles up. Then they start dancing and Mrs Everett sings 'Red sails in the sunset'.

FRIDAY: Last day of term. Hooray again! Arrange with Alice to meet up and go swimming next week.

Back home it's really crowded. We can't get back into the house for another three months. I don't mind. I'm happy. Mum and Dad are in our old room. Tommy and I sleep in living room on inflatable mattresses HAPPY Kenny has lent us. It's cool. I can wait.

Chapter 22

"Come on – let's all go out," said Dad on Saturday morning. "Give Gran some peace. What's on today?"

I heard myself saying, "There's a Horse Show." I don't know why I said it – it just popped into my head.

So here we were, in a field on the edge of town, along with about half my class, who had come to watch Venetia.

"Mr Pike! Mrs Pike! We thought you'd been eaten by a whale!" It was Mickey Grimshaw. "Can I have your autograph?"

He was followed by a whole lot of kids, jumping up and down and holding out programmes for

Mum and Dad to sign. I supposed belonging to a famous family was quite cool; I wasn't sure. I edged away.

The Horse Show was in full swing. Small girls and boys on ponies trotted round, while their parents called out things like "Come on, Sebastian!" and "Keep her steady, Felicity!" Other kids were grooming their ponies or changing into riding gear.

At last it was time for the bigger ponies and the older children. The ponies wheeled and turned; their manes and tails were plaited and their bodies gleamed in the sunshine. They and their riders made a lot of mistakes, though; they kept knocking over poles, colliding with hedges and refusing to jump. One or two of the riders fell off.

A whisper went round – "It's Venetia!" – and all the kids forgot about autographs and ran to the railings.

Venetia sat astride Sultan, waiting her turn. She wore a riding hat, jacket and jodhpurs and a haughty expression. Sultan looked fantastic. He was brown and glossy and he snorted and pawed the ground.

The gate opened.

"Go, Venetia, go!" cried Simon and Sylvia.

And Venetia wasn't half bad, though I say it myself. She soared over hedges and fences like a bird. The final jump was a wall made of wooden bricks. Sultan cleared it easily and there was a storm of clapping. Venetia rode back with her nose in the air.

Mum and Tommy went off to queue for ice creams; Dad had met some old friends and disappeared into the crowd. I wandered off behind a clump of trees. I just wanted to be alone. I thought about Blue – about all the nice things he'd done for me and how I was going to miss him. And, suddenly, without warning, there he was. He'd come without being called. He fizzled into shape in front of me.

"Blue!" I said. "I thought you'd gone forever."

"Mm. Not quite," said Blue. "I had to come back. I've got one last treat for you, Cowslip."

"What is it?" I asked suspiciously.

"What's the thing you've always wished for?" asked Blue.

"For Mum and Dad to come back," I said. "And now they have."

"There was something else," said Blue.

I looked blank.

"Cowslip Pike!" said Blue. "I'm offering you the chance of a lifetime! The chance to show off in front of your friends. The chance to ride a magnificent horse."

"Where is he?" I said, looking round.

"Here!" trumpeted Blue. "Here, of course. It's me, silly!"

I was silent. I was very fond of Blue, but — I ask you! "A magnificent horse?" Hardly.

"Perhaps this will help you make up your mind," said Blue and he took a deep breath. He shivered and shook all over and then, before my very eyes, he began to change. He grew and he grew. His colour deepened to dark blue, and then to navy blue, until at last it was blue-black, like ink. He let his breath out with a "Phew!"

"What do you think?" he asked.

I was lost for words. There before me was a Blue I'd never seen before — a tall, noble animal with an arched neck, a strong back and a swishing mane and tail. *Exactly* the sort of horse I'd dreamed about riding into the playground.

He was fully saddled up and on his saddle rested a riding hat and a jacket with a "Number Ten" on the back.

"You'd better put these on," he said.

It was an offer I couldn't refuse. I know a true heroine would have said "No. I don't need to prove myself to anyone. But thanks for asking."

But I wasn't a true heroine, was I? And I was into that riding gear and up into the saddle before you could say "Cowslip Pike."

There was one more thing.

"But Blue," I said. "No-one will see us."

"For one performance only!" whinnyed Blue. "I am on view! I'm treating everyone today! Now, Cowslip – don't let me down. Keep a straight back and hang on to the reins. I'll do the rest."

And with that, we were off, trotting towards the ring.

Chapter 23

"We have two clear rounds!" the announcer was saying. "Number Seven and Number Ten. Now it's a race against the clock."

That was Venetia and – hang on! Number Ten? That was me and Blue! How had that happened? We hadn't even ridden in the first round, had we?

"First to go! Number Seven!" said the announcer.

A bell rang and Venetia was off. She sped around the course, clearing everything until all that was left was the wall. She raced towards it. "Oh!" gasped the crowd as she soared upwards; and "Ah!" they groaned as Sultan's rear foot clipped one of the top bricks and knocked it off. Venetia cantered back; she looked furious.

"And now – Number Ten!" said the announcer.

Venetia was standing next to Sultan, a scowl on her face. As we trotted past, her mouth dropped open and her eyes stood out on stalks. Oh yes! Result!

The gate opened, the bell rang and we were off. I could hear cries as we cantered up to the first fence.

"Look! It's Cowslip! Cowslip Pike!"

"She *has* got a horse!"

"Wow!"

The cries faded as I began to concentrate. We were about to jump. I held my breath and over we went. We speeded up. Ditches, fences, hedges – they were all a piece of cake to Blue. I tried to keep a straight back and leaned forward when we jumped like I'd seen the others do. Blue turned at all the right places, judged his

distances just right and sailed over everything
like a swallow. The wall loomed up before us.

"Hold on!" whispered Blue. "I'm going for it!"
and before he had finished speaking we were
up and over.

Blue wheeled round and cantered back to
the finishing line. He pranced about, swishing
his tail and there was a storm of clapping and

cheering. Venetia was still standing there with her mouth open.

"A clear round for Number Ten!" cried the announcer. "And the fastest time! We have a winner!"

Blue was muttering to himself.

"Those jumps are for wimps!" I heard him say.

Then he wheeled round again. The applause died away and turned to gasps as Blue broke into a gallop and thundered down the course. When he reached the far end he did an enormous leap and sailed over the heads of the crowd. People screamed and ducked, but they need not have worried – we cleared them with miles to spare. We galloped on and Blue only slowed down when we were well out of sight. We skidded to a halt behind some horse boxes at the far end of the field.

I slid off.

"Blue!" I cried. "What are you doing? I want my rosette!"

Blue was panting.

"Don't you think you've done enough?" he asked.

I was silent.

"You've shown Venetia," said Blue. "And everyone else. Isn't that enough for you?"

I thought for a moment. Blue was right. After all, it *was* all his own work, wasn't it? I could do without a rosette.

"Anyway, Cowslip," said Blue. "Your time's up. It's goodbye time."

I flung my arms round his neck.

"Don't go, Blue!" I cried.

"I've got to," said Blue. "Bye-bye, Cowslip. It was nice knowing you."

And even as he spoke, he started to fade – from black to navy and then to light blue, and I could see the horse-box through his shimmering body.

"Blue – *thank you!*" I cried.

There was a sound like lemonade fizzing. Then I was left clutching thin air and he was gone. And so was my riding gear.

Just in time. Mickey Grimshaw and some of the others came pounding round the corner.

"Cowslip!" panted Mickey. "Where's your horse?"

"He's gone," I said, telling the truth for once. "Perhaps you imagined him."

"No way!" said Alec Johnson. "That horse was real!"

"Where did you learn to ride like that, Cowslip?" asked Lizzie. "You were wonderful!"

I walked back, surrounded by a little crowd. In the ring, Venetia was just going up to receive her prize. It seemed Blue and I had been disqualified for racing down the course and running off. I didn't mind at all. It was cool. Venetia didn't look too happy about it, though; she had a face like thunder on her.

"There you are, Cowslip," said my Mum, holding out a dripping cone with a flake in it. "Where have you been?"

"She's been riding her horse, Mrs Pike!" said Mickey Grimshaw. "She was great!"

"'Riding her horse'?" said Mum, putting her head on one side and looking at me strangely. "I wonder where he came from – out of the blue?"

chapter 24

So, folks – that's it! Almost it, anyway. Tommy was safe, Mum and Dad were home – what more could anyone want? And yet – I *had* got more. I'd ridden a fantastic horse, everyone had seen me doing it and they were all calling me Cowslip again. Respect! And the day wasn't quite over yet. Here's how it ended.

4 o'clock: Find Dad and get ready to leave. Pass Venetia, Simon and Sylvia loading Sultan into a horse-box. Venetia glares. Says, "You ride like a sack of potatoes, Cowslip." I say, "Thanks, Venetia. You were pretty good, too."

4.30: Walking down High Street. Mum says, "Well, there's one more person who deserves a happy ending, isn't there?" steers us into Mark's Ark, the pet shop. We choose a new budgie for Gran. Dad says, "He's the dead spit of Bobby Six, isn't he?" Not so sure.

Hallo! I'm Bobby 7

5.30: Up in the lift. Find Gran watching TV. Surprise, surprise. Give her the bird. Pretends to be delighted and puts him in cage. Tommy starts to teach him to say, "Hallo! I'm Bobby Seven!"

6 o'clock: Something tumbles through window and flutters down onto TV. Chirrups, "Who's a pretty boy, then?". "Bobby!" shrieks Gran. "It's Bobby Six! He's come home!" Picks him up and starts kissing him. Now she has two budgies. Obviously her lucky day.

Behind Gran, something catches my eye. It's a blue shadow. It passes across the window and then it's gone.

THE END